Kat and Juju

written and illustrated by
Kataneh Vahdani

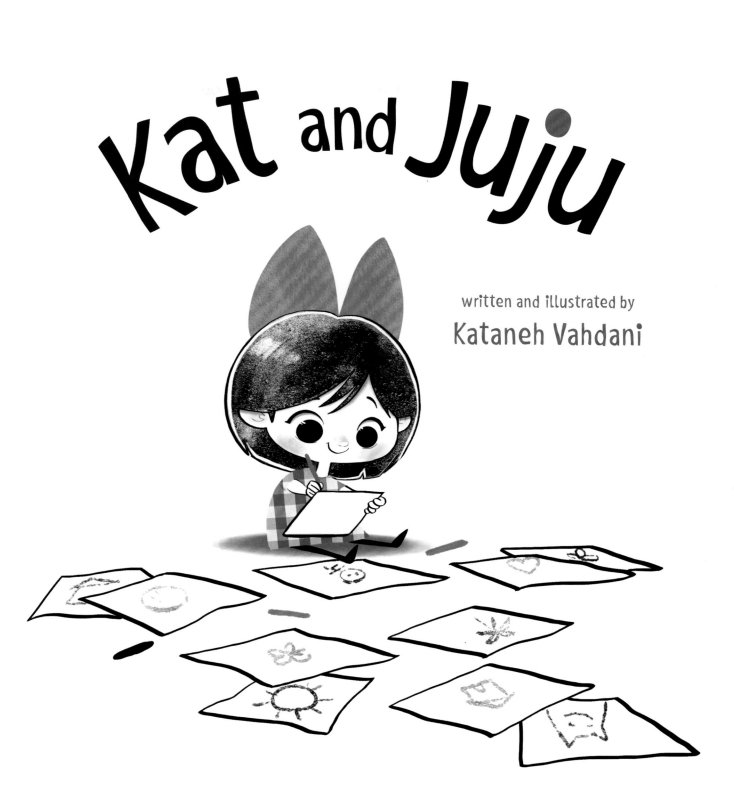

two lions

Published by Two Lions, New York
www.apub.com

Amazon, the Amazon logo, and Two Lions are trademarks
of Amazon.com, Inc., or its affiliates.

ISBN-13: 9781542043281
ISBN-10: 154204328X

The illustrations were created digitally.
Graphic design by Tanya Ross-Hughes

Printed in China
First Edition
10 9 8 7 6 5 4 3 2 1

تقدیم به پرنده جوجو که به من یاد داد شجاع باشم و به
مادر مهربونم که به من اجازه داد روی دیوارها نقاشی کنم.

Dedicated to my Juju bird who helped me be brave and
to my kind mother who allowed me to draw on walls.

Kat liked to do things her very own way.

When she colored, she always stayed inside the lines.

She found wonder in places no one else thought to look.

Sometimes she told her secrets to trees.
They never told anyone what she said.

Nobody knows but you.

She knew the other kids
wondered about her, but she was
too shy to talk to them.

Sometimes she got lonely....

Kat couldn't wait for her next birthday.
That's when her very best friend would arrive.
At least that's what had happened for all the other kids.

It would be the best birthday present in . . . ever!

On the morning of her birthday,

Kat bounced down the stairs.

Kat knew that she and Juju were definitely
going to be very best friends.

Juju was silly and had a big laugh.
He colored outside the lines.

He saw things differently than she did.

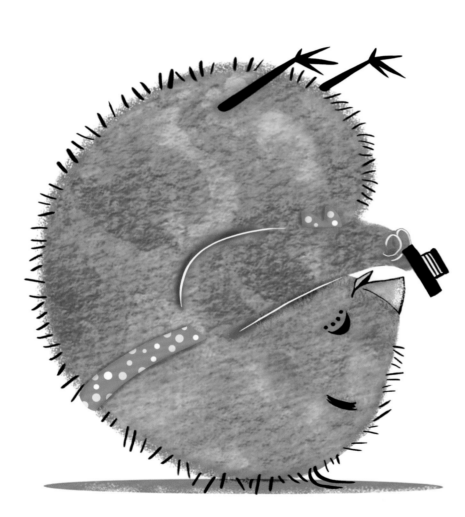

Nothing seemed to frighten him.

Kat wondered if he would still like her.

Juju stayed by Kat's side.
He tried to help her to be brave.

Sometimes
you've just got to
LET GO

and do
a HAPPY DANCE.

Kat wished she could.

But what if everyone laughed?

Juju didn't care what others thought.
He just kept on dancing.

Until something made him stop.

The birdie looked frightened.
Kat knew what that was like.

Don't be scared.
I am here.

With Juju's help, Kat nursed the birdie back to health.

One day that will be YOU!

Bit by bit, the birdie got stronger.
But it was still too scared to fly.
Kat tried everything she could to help.

Even when it was hard.

One day, something wonderful happened.
The birdie was brave enough to fly on its own.

And then something even more
surprising happened.

For a moment, Kat stopped worrying about what everyone else thought.

And that made her happy.
Kat still did things her very own way . . .

but she wasn't lonely anymore.